LEO and EMILY and the DRAGON

by FRANZ BRANDENBERG
illustrated by ALIKI

Greenwillow Books · New York

Library of Congress Cataloging in Publication Data
Brandenberg, Franz.   Leo and Emily and the dragon.
(Greenwillow read-alone books)
Summary: Leo and Emily pack their rucksacks
and hike in search of a dragon. Later that
evening, they repack their rucksacks and hike
again with their baby sitter.
[1. Hiking—Fiction.   2. Baby sitters—Fiction]
I. Aliki, ill.   II. Title.   III. Series.
PZ7.B7364 Leg 1984   [E]   83-14091
ISBN 0-688-02531-5   ISBN 0-688-02532-3 (lib. bdg.)

for Caroline and Matthew Harada

CONTENTS

CHAPTER ONE
THE HUNT

"Let's go catch a dragon,"
said Emily.

"That's a good idea," said Leo.

"Where can we find one?"

"In a cave, I guess," said Emily.

"How do we find a cave?"
asked Leo.

"We'll go look for one,"
said Emily.

"What do we need?" asked Leo.

"A net to catch the dragon,"
said Emily.

"And flashlights," said Leo.

"And raincoats in case it rains,"
said Emily.

"And bathing suits in case we
  pass a lake on the way," said Leo.
"And suntan lotion," said Emily.
"And sandwiches," said Leo.
"And blankets to sit on,"
  said Emily.

"And sleeping bags to take
a nap," said Leo.
"And knapsacks to put
everything in," said Emily.
"And hiking shoes," said Leo.
"We'll meet in an hour
in our garden," said Emily.
"All right," said Leo.

"I have everything,"
said Emily.

"So do I," said Leo.

"Don't go too far,"
called Emily's mother.

"We won't," said Emily.

"Be back before dark,"
called Leo's father.

"We will," said Leo.

"My knapsack is very heavy,"
said Emily.

"So is mine," said Leo. "Perhaps
we could take something out."

"But what?" said Emily. "Let's
have a look."

"Mine is full of food," said Leo.

"So is mine," said Emily.

"That's what's heavy," said Leo.

"What can we do about it?"
asked Emily.

"We could eat it," said Leo.
"Not before we have caught
  the dragon," said Emily.
"Work before pleasure."
"If we ate it now,
  we'd be much stronger
  to catch the dragon,"
  said Leo.
"And the knapsacks
  would be so much lighter,"
  said Emily.

They spread out the blankets,
and had a picnic.
When they had eaten all the food,
they put their knapsacks back on.
"It's still heavy," said Leo.
"It's those sleeping bags,"
said Emily.
"If we took our naps now, we could
leave them here," said Leo.
"First we catch the dragon,
then we nap," said Emily.
"If we napped now, we'd be fresh
and rested for the hunt," said Leo.

"Actually, all that food made me sleepy," said Emily.
They unrolled their sleeping bags, and crawled in.

When they woke up,

the sun was going down.

"It's time to go home," said Leo.

"We brought the net for nothing,"

said Emily.

"Another time," said Leo.

"We could have left our bathing suits
at home," said Emily.
"There is still some sun," said Leo.
They put on their bathing suits,
and rubbed each other with
suntan lotion.

They lay down on the blankets.
"It's getting cold," said Emily.
They got dressed.

"We could have done without
our raincoats," said Emily.
"There is always the garden hose,"
said Leo.
They put on their raincoats,
and hosed each other down.

"We didn't need the flashlights,"
said Emily.
"If we wait a few minutes,
we will," said Leo.
It was getting dark.
They packed their knapsacks,
and put them on.
They lit their flashlights,
and made their way home.

"How was the hike?"
asked Emily's mother.
"It was fun," said Emily.
"The food was delicious,"
said Leo.

"You must be tired from carrying those heavy knapsacks," said Emily's father.

"We were glad we had them," said Emily.

"We used every single thing we brought."

"You deserve a good night's sleep,"
said Emily's mother.
"But not yet," said Leo.
"Could Leo stay awhile, please?"
asked Emily.

"He can stay all night,"
said her father. "We are going out
with his parents."
"Who is babysitting?" asked Leo.
"Harold," said Emily's mother.

CHAPTER TWO
THE BABYSITTER

"Harold is boring!" said Leo.
"All he ever does is raid
    the refrigerator and watch TV."
"And he is getting paid for it,"
    said Emily. "Tonight we'll
    make him earn his money."

As soon as their parents had left,
Leo and Emily got out of bed.
They went into the living room.
Harold was sitting in front
of the TV.

"You are supposed to be
in bed," he said.
"We aren't sleepy,"
said Leo and Emily.

"Aren't you tired from your
big hike?" asked Harold.
"I feel as fresh as a daisy,"
said Emily.
"I could go on another hike
right now," said Leo.
"Could I come, too?"
asked Harold.

"Do you have a knapsack?"
asked Emily.

"And hiking shoes?" asked Leo.

"And a bathing suit, a raincoat,
suntan lotion, a blanket,
a sleeping bag, and a flashlight?"

"And sandwiches?" asked Emily.

"I don't," said Harold.

"But I'll help you carry yours."

"All right, you can come,"
said Emily.

Leo and Emily repacked their
knapsacks, and put them on.

Harold carried the blankets
and sleeping bags.

"Do you know a cave?"
asked Leo.

"Of course," said Harold.

"Follow me!"

He led them into the dark
dining room.

"Look at those stalactites,"
said Leo, shining his flashlight
at the chandelier.

"And those bats," said Emily,
pointing at the shadows
on the ceiling.

"What's that?" whispered Harold,
staring across the room.

A pair of fiery eyes was glowing
in the dark.

41

"A dragon!" said Leo.

"Get out the net!" said Emily.

"It's at the bottom of the knapsack,"
 said Leo.

"I am getting out of here,"
 said Harold, in a trembling voice.

"So am I," said Leo.

"You cowards, it's only the cat,"
said Emily, shining her flashlight
at it.
Harold and Leo sighed with relief.
They went back
to the living room.

"It's good to see the sun again,"
said Leo.

"I think we deserve a swim," said Emily.
She and Leo put on their bathing suits.

"I won't come into the water,"
said Harold. "I'll just watch."
Leo and Emily swam across
the polished living room floor.

Then they lay on their blankets.
Harold rubbed them
with suntan lotion.
When they had sunbathed enough,
they got up.

"Perhaps you better take a shower
before you get dressed," said Harold.
"To wash off the salt."
Leo and Emily went
to take a shower.

"It's raining again," said Leo.
"A good thing we brought our
raincoats," said Emily.

"Hurry up, and get dressed!"
called Harold.
"Why?" asked Leo and Emily.
"Because in five minutes my
favorite TV program
comes on,"
said Harold.

"But we haven't had our picnic yet,"
said Emily.

"We forgot to pack sandwiches,"
said Leo.

"We could raid the refrigerator,"
said Emily.

"I'll take care of that," said Harold.
Leo and Emily quickly dressed,
and settled on their blankets
in front of the TV.
Harold arrived with the food.
"Ice cream, hurrah!"
shouted the children.

"Thank you for raiding the
refrigerator for us," said Emily.
"And for letting us watch TV,"
said Leo.
"Thank you for letting me come
on your hike,"
said Harold.

"That dragon really
wore me out," said Leo.
"I am ready for a nap."
"So am I," said Emily.

Harold zipped them into
their sleeping bags.
"Harold isn't that boring,"
said Leo.
"Harold is fun!" said Emily.
"What a great day!" said Leo.
"I can't wait for tomorrow!"
said Emily.
But Leo didn't answer.
He was fast asleep.

FRANZ and ALIKI BRANDENBERG are
husband and wife. They have collaborated on two
other books about these two special friends —
Leo and Emily and *Leo and Emily's Big Ideas.*
They have also produced a group of books about
a cat family — *A Secret for Grandmother's
Birthday, A Robber! A Robber!, I Wish I Was Sick,
Too!,* and *A Picnic, Hurrah!,* and several books
about a Fieldmouse family, which include *What
Can You Make of It?, Nice New Neighbors, Six New
Students,* and *It's Not My Fault.*

Franz and Aliki have a son, Jason, and a
daughter, Alexa, who are neither cats nor mice.
They are teenagers.